ISBN: 979-8-218-07504-0

## Dedication

For Jemma and Corey Jr.

# Carter the Quiet and the Missing Mask

# Written by Jasmine Elise Smith

**Carter, stop! Don't forget your mask?**

**Before you leave home, do this task.**

Carter the Quiet could stay out all day. He loved nothing more than to run and play.

He would jog through the fields with no care at all—
and would climb any hill that wasn't too small.

He loved the feeling of sun on his skin,
and would dance at sunset—
to delay going in.

The park was his playground—he would climb trees, on repeat.

Carter tried to make friends, by waving on the street.

But his mask was missing, and he had to stand back—
so, kids he couldn't meet, and friends he did lack.

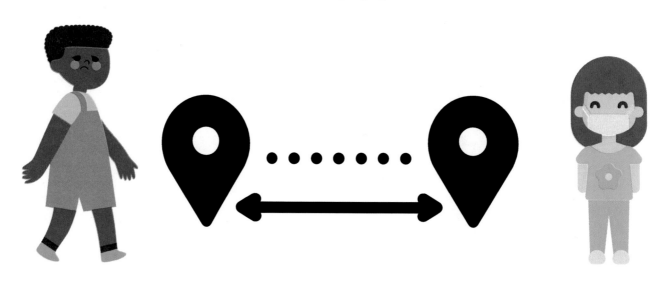

6 feet

But was the mask missing?

No! Carter was pretending.
He was tired of his family, constantly recommending.

But he hated his mask!
He thought his words would be trapped—

in this new world, he could not adapt.

So, Carter stayed home—
feeling alone, while his sister was in school.

He would sit there so quiet, reading books in silence—
when the weather was too cool.

He would spend the day thinking, he didn't fit in—
without a friend, or a mask on his chin.
This was a battle; he just couldn't win.

It was hopeless and sad—
and boy, did he feel bad...watching the days go by!

He began to imagine, a time without masks, and all the places he'd try...

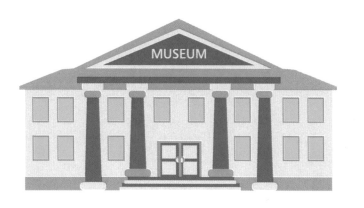

...like big museums, birthday parties, or even a building up high!

That was it!
Carter couldn't just sit and miss the fun any longer.

He decided to give in, practice wearing his mask, so his tolerance could grow stronger.

Carter tried and tried, but the mask felt wrong.
The rules were lasting too long!

Enough was enough, he was in a rut.
In the house, he had to stay shut.

No more forcing the mask on his face!
Maybe it should disappear, without a trace.

Put it on, now!

It didn't make sense, masks made him so tense.
He had to go his own pace.

Just when Carter gave up,
in his fears he was stuck—
a new mask, he did find.

He looked in the mirror and,
WOW, he changed his mind!

The heroes he saw, showed him
true courage—combined.

**They all wore masks! He could be like them!**
**His future was no longer dim.**

Now, Carter plays with lots of friends,
and has a new school, that he attends.

His mask gives him courage, it keeps him well.
This new view, helped him come out of his shell.

So the case is closed, and everyone knows, that Carter just wanted total control.

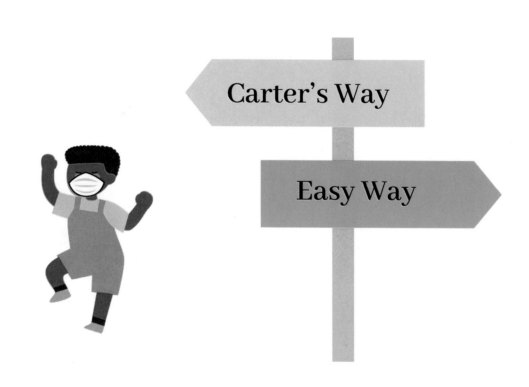

## About the Author

Jasmine Elise Smith wrote *Carter the Quiet and the Missing Mask* for her own little ones, who have had to navigate the pandemic, masks and all. She has a passion for reading, writing, and educating future leaders. Jasmine lives in Michigan with her husband, Corey, and their kids, Jemma and Corey Jr.

## A Word by the Author

If you enjoyed this book, continue the Carter series by reading my first book,
*Carter the Quiet and the Curious Chaos.*
Please leave a review on Amazon.
Share on Facebook, Instagram, and Twitter.
Contact me at carterthequiet@gmail.com.

# Acknowledgments

© Front Cover, Pages: 1-24, Back Cover, Turquoise Green Children's Book Day Instagram Post Template by Reallygreatsite via Canva.com, Items included in design:

- © Front Cover, Cloud by djvstock via Canva.com
- © Front Cover, Flying Pink Bird by Rafiico Studio via Canva.com
- © Front Cover, tree by purwakawebid from pixabay via Canva.com
- © Front Cover, Grass Vector by THP Creative via Canva.com

© Front Cover, Pages: 3-11, 13, 15-22, Back Cover, Character Builder by Canva via Canva.com

© Front Cover, Page 21, Children kids wearing a face mask to get vaccine character. by Felizlalala from Felizlalala via Canva.com

© Page 3, Recycle Bin by Icons8 via Canva.com

© Pages: 3-4, 9, 16, 18, Medical Mask Icon by iXimus from pixabay via Canva.com

© Page 4, Blue Front Door by studiog2 via Canva.com

© Page 5, Circle Frame by Canva via Canva.com

© Page 6, Backyard Fence and Lights by vecstock via Canva.com

© Page 7, Park Tree Lamp Post Road Nature by gstudioimagen2 via Canva.com

© Pages: 7, 9, Mask by ouch via Canva.com

© Pages: 7-8, girl wearing face mask by nes_kanyanee from Nes Kanyanee via Canva.com

© Page 8, Distances by codenamerahul via Canva.com

© Page 10, Simple Organic Door Flashcard by Sketchify Education via Canva.com

© Pages: 10 and 17, No mask no entry sign with cartoon character by BRGFX via Canva.com

© Pages: 10 and 18, Thinking Speech Bubble by Farikha Rosyida via Canva.com

© Page 11, Workroom scene with a laptop on the table by Matthew Cole's Images via Canva.com

© Page 12, cloud bubble by Sarwono from FeatherpenCS via Canva.com

© Page 12, School icon by Aimagenarium via Canva.com

© Page 12, Kids Wearing Face Masks and Doing an Elbow Bump Illustration by ann131313.c via Canva.com

© Page 12, Respect Gesture Illustration by ann131313.c via Canva.com

© Page 13, Apartment Window Scenery by sketchify via Canva.com

© Page 13, 3D Kids Student Classroom Chair by Drawcee via Canva.com

© Page 14, Blocky Flat Buildable Museum by Sketchify Education via Canva.com

© Page 14, Birthday Party Festive Cartoon by yupiramos via Canva.com

© Page 14, Building by ferdizzimo via Canva.com

© Page 15, School Bus Illustration by BilliTheCat from pixabay via Canva.com

© Page 15, Sidewalk Icon, Cartoon Style by ivandesign via Canva.com

© Page 17, Outlined Girl Getting Her Temperature Checked by Sketchify Education via Canva.com

© Page 17, Stay Home Icon by Wanicon via Canva.com

© Page 19, Sleek Gradient Geometric Mirror by Trendify via Canva.com

© Pages: 19-20, Clean Vector Young Male Doctor with Face Mask by sketchify via Canva.com

© Pages: 19-20, African nurse with light bulb by cottidie from Katja via Canva.com

© Pages: 19-20, Dentist by rafyfane via Canva.com

© Pages: 19-22, and Back Cover, Medical Mask by ouch via Canva.com

© Page 20, hospital by Twemoji via Canva.com

© Page 20, dentist office by Roundicons Pro via Canva.com

© Page 22, Choice by Studio 365 via Canva.com